THE FREAKY WOODS OF THE DARK

GURU PRASAD SWAIN

The freaky woods of the dark

The forest was quiet this morning walking with my dog, jack. The sound of a slight wind in the trees, cries of birds, and the patter of jack's paws on the forest floor running here and there sniffing, and rushing after small animals. Those small animals always seem faster than jack and get the better of her. Off in the distance we heard the church bells rung eight of the clocks. We were a little later than normal when we set out. A mist was rising in places, from last night's rain. Cool, the humidity began to bead. I stepped over piles of leaf litter and cones washed throughout the path in piles. Looking at the streams, they seemed excited, dancing over the rocks. Coming between a couple of large boulders supporting tall, waving trees whose roots gripped like fingers to the rock, we saw an old man. The smoke from his small pipe drifted upward as he sat on a rock. I noticed his clothing was unusual. The path led us to the man; as we approached, jack little wary but tail wagging, he looked up and smiled. After a friendly greeting we began to talk. "My wife will be along soon," he said. "She's a wonderful woman. She loves dogs. She'll like this one." The man scratched jacks' ear as she got closer to gingerly sniff his trousers. "Is she a mutt?" I told him what I believed was jacks varied ancestry. We discussed that the day was quite beautiful despite the mist, maybe because of it and how this was such a nice place to wander. I asked how he had met his wife. She saved me, she did." I asked him, how? "From a bird," he said and took a puff on his pipe, the smoke once more gently rising towards the branches drooping above us. I wasn't sure what to say, so I sat down on a fallen tree and listened.

"We lived in a small cottage in a small town where we told stories to small children. Sometimes when it rained in the summer, we would come here and we'd dance beneath the showering clouds and dripping trees. Too old for that now, I think." I smiled. "We grew together," he said. "Aged together, and joked about each other farting. Hers were sweeter than mine, and she always let me know! We always held hands, except when we were cooking together, or reading. Sometimes we'd write poems to each other and hide them so we'd find them later. It was more than once when I hid mine too well and would have to unhide them." I couldn't help but laugh at this. I turned about to see between the branches. There was still no sign of the man wife. wondered at what type of person she was. They were obviously happy together. Geese flew overhead, and I looked up. Their cries filled the air. Jack jumped about, then spotting a squirrel chased after it. "Lively one, that dog of yours." "She is that. Her name jack" "What, for Maureen?" "No, just jack. J A C K." "She likes the woods, err?" I nodded. "She does." There was still no sign of his wife.

"jack loves most places I take her," I told the man. He looked over his shoulder, then turning back opened a pocket watch that appeared in his hand. Gazing at the watch face, he shrugged. The watch looked old but well kept, the kind I wouldn't mind owning one day. He lifted his face and spoke. "We loved going to town market. It always seemed an adventure. The market sellers were always smiling at us. It was as if we were rich and they wanted us to spend all our money on them. But they knew we weren't. We had fun tasting the wares, though, especially if they had chocolates. It was rare they 'ad chocolates, though. If the old bookseller was at the market, we would sit and read bits of books and stories to each other, buying our favourite to read at home together later. "My favourite was when one of townspeople would visit and play the fiddle for us. I was getting on then. We would slowly dance in each other's arms, eventually collapsing on the sofa and we'd fall asleep still wrapped in an embrace." The man smiled and gazed off, as if remembering something from a long time ago. "One o' me friends said our kisses could light the skies, that fireflies glowed more brightly when me and the missus kissed, the crickets would chirp louder, and birds sing more sweetly! At least that's what he said." The old man looked about again. He sighed. "Seems she's not coming today. Maybe tomorrow." He sat gently tapping his pipe on the rock, watching the tobacco fall to the forest floor. Lifting a foot, he stamped the tobacco out in the damp earth. "Oh well. I hope I didn't bore. I don't get to meet too many folks who notice me out here in the woods. Folk are funny these days it seems. Won't even look in the eye." "You didn't bother me at all. It's nice to meet you. A pleasure. I should get on though. Work and all that." I turned and called for jack, who came bounding towards me and leaped up on the rock the old man and been sitting on. The old man had vanished. I stared at jack. It was then I realized that the man had only talked in the past tense. I looked at where the burned tobacco had fallen, & sniffed the air, but could see no sign of it nor smell the tobacco. It occurred to me that he had never told me his name, nor how his wife. fog surrounding me and my two best friends was thick, the air muggy and all sense of the world gone. As we walked on further into the woods it was difficult to know both where we were going and when we would get there. Fear was pounding at my heart, but there was no going back. I had to keep going. Me and my two best friends' mile and mina, pushed forward struggling to breathe as we went. The track seemed to be endless. There was nowhere to go. We were lost in the middle of a dark forest with no food no water, shelter, that was when we started to panic. My breath started to stager. It was too hard to keep going. My knees went weak and gave way. It felt as though I was falling. Falling through a deep tunnel. I had fainted. I woke up shortly after with mile slapping my face painfully and shacking me. A look of concern crossed with fear was upon mina face. I tried to sit up but the pain in my stomach was unbearable. Finally, I was able to sit up against the tree. Though as I sat the three of us remained silent. Up further away a wolf cried to the moon. Which was barley, visible through the dense fog. It was hard to tell who was more scared. The looks on mile's and Mina face made me feel very uneasy. We sat there for a minute that seemed to go for an eternity. As the trees moved in the aggressive wind, shadows of fighting shapes littered the ground. As we moved on, we came to a house. Which was very odd in such a deserted nature, we approached carefully not wanting any animals to know that we were walking in their land on. Their territory in which they guard viciously and greedily wanting to protect them their families and the place in which the protect greedily. As we approached, a wolf ran in front of us. Its blood red eyes were boring into us. We started to back away but there was no way where to go. The wolf gave us a fleeting look that told us it would be back. I looked into mile's soft hazel eyes then into mina with blue eyes. We walked on. Finally, we reached the house. Smoke was rising from a chimney and drifting softly into the air without a care in the world. I knocked. There was a ringing silence that went for a time that seemed to want to last forever. No one answered.

I knocked again. A groaning noise came from within and a young beautiful woman steeped out. We were saved. She let us her phone. Ten minutes later a midnight blue care was speeding towards us. To rescue us. The journey home was enjoyable with a nice long nap. Everything was back to normal again. moving his feet because he had nothing else to do, peter went on down the road, hating the trees that moved slowly against his progress, hating the dust beneath his feet, hating the sky, hating this road, all roads, everywhere. He had been walking since morning, and all day the day before that, and the day before that, and days before that, back into the numberless line of walking days that dissolved, seemingly years ago, into the place he had left, once, before he started walking. This morning he had been walking past fields, and now he was walking past trees that mounted heavily to the road, and leaned across, bending their great old bodies toward him; peter had come into the forest at a crossroads, turning onto the forest road as though he had a choice, looking back once to see the other road, the one he had not chosen, going peacefully on through fields, in and out of towns, perhaps even coming to an end somewhere beyond peter sight. The cat had joined him shortly after he entered the forest, emerging from between the trees in a quick, shadowy movement that surprised peter at first and then, oddly, comforted him, and the cat had stayed beside him, moving closer to peter as the trees pressed insistently closer to them both, trotting along in the casual acceptance of human company that cats exhibit when they are frightened. Peter, when he stopped once to rest, sitting on a large stone at the edge of the road, had rubbed the cat's ears and pulled the cat's tail affectionately, and had said, "Where we going,? and the cat had closed his eyes meaningfully and opened them again. "Haven't seen a house since we came into these trees," peter remarked once, later, to the cat; seeing up at the sky, he had added, "it is Going to be dark before long." He glanced apprehensively at the trees so close to him, irritated by the sound of his own voice in the silence, as though the trees were listening to him and, listening, had nodded solemnly to one another. "Don't worry," peter said to the cat. "Road's got to go somewhere." It was not much later—an hour before dark, probably—that peter and the cat paused, surprised, at a turn in the road, because a house was ahead. A neat stone fence ran down to the road, smoke came naturally from the chimneys, the doors and windows were not nailed shut, nor were the steps broken or the hinges sagging. It was a comfortable-looking, settled old house, made of stone like its fence, easily found in the pathless forest because it lay correctly, compactly, at the end of the road, which was not a road at all, of course, but merely a way to the house. Peter thought briefly of the other way, long before, that he had not followed, and then moved forward, the cat at his heels, to the front door of the house. The sound of a river came from among the trees that pressed closely against the sides of the house; the river knew a way out of the forest, because it moved along sweetly and clearly, over clean stones and, unafraid, among the dark trees. peter approached the house as he would any house, farmhouse, or city apartment, and knocked politely and with pleasure on the warm front door. "Come in, then," a woman said as she opened it, and peter stepped inside, followed closely by the cat. The woman stood back and looked for a minute at peter, her eyes searching and wide; he looked back at her and saw that she was young, not so young as he would have liked, but too young, seemingly, to be living in the heart of a forest. "I've been here for a long time, though," she said, as though she read his thoughts. Out of this dark hallway, he thought, she might look older; her hair curled a little around her face, and her eyes were far too wide for the rest of her, as if she were constantly straining to see in the gloom of the forest. She wore a long green dress that was gathered at her waist by a belt made of what he subsequently saw was grass woven into a rope; she was barefoot. While he stood uneasily just inside the door, looking at her as she looked at him, the cat went round the hall, stopping curiously at corners and before closed doors, glancing up, once, into the unlighted heights of the stairway that rose from the far end of the hall. "He smells another cat," she said. "We have one." a voice called from the back of the house, and the woman smiled quickly, nervously, at peter and said, "Come along, please. I shouldn't keep you waiting." He followed her to the door at the back of the hall, next to the stairway, and was grateful for the light that greeted them when she opened it. It led directly into a great warm kitchen, glowing with an open fire on its heart, and well lit, against the late-afternoon dimness of the forest, by three kerosene lamps set on table and shelves. A second woman stood by the stove, watching the pots that steamed and smelled garlic and herbs; peter closed his eyes, like the cat, against the unbelievable beauty of warmth, light, and the smell of garlic. "Well," the woman at the stove said with finality, turning to look at peter. She studied him carefully, as the other woman had done, and then turned her eyes to a bare whitewashed area, high on the kitchen wall, where lines and crosses indicated a rough measuring system. "Another day," she said. "What's your name?" the first woman asked peter, and he said "peter" without effort and then, "What's yours?" the young woman said. "What's your cat's name?" "I don't know," peter said. He smiled a little. "It's not even my cat," he went on, his voice gathering strength from the smell of the garlic. "He just followed me here." "We'll have to name him something," When she spoke, she looked away from peter, turning her overlarge eyes on him again only when she stopped speaking. "Our cat's named Grime." "Grime," Christopher said. "Her name, gesturing toward the cook with her head. "Her name's Aunt Cissy." "sima," the older woman said doggedly to the stove. "sima was born and will have for my name till I die." Although she seemed, from the way she stood and the way she kept her voice to a single note, to be much older actually, when peter saw her face clearly in the light of the lamps she was as vigorous and clear-eyed, and the strength in her arms when she lifted the great iron pot easily off the stove and carried it to the stone table in the centre of the kitchen surprised peter. The cat, who had followed peter into the kitchen, leaped noiselessly onto the bench beside the table, and then onto the table; looked warily at peter for a minute before she pushed the cat gently to drive him off the table. "We'll have to find a name for your cat," she said apologetically as the cat leaped down without taking offense. "Kitty," peter said helplessly. "I guess I always call cats kitty." She was about to speak when Aunt sima stopped her with a glance, and moved quickly to an iron chest in the corner of the kitchen, from which she took a cloth to spread on the table, and heavy stone plates and mugs, which she set on the table in four places. peter sat down on the bench, with his back to the table, to indicate clearly that he had no intention of presuming that he was sitting at the table but was only on the bench because he was tired, that he would not swing around to the table until invited warmly and specifically to do so. "Are we almost ready, then?" Aunt sima said. She swept her eyes across the table, adjusted a fork, and stood back, her glance never for a minute resting on peter. Then she moved over to the wall beside the door, where she stood, quiet and erect, and went to stand beside her. peter, turning his head to look at them, had to turn again as footsteps approached from the hall, and, after a minute's interminable pause, the door opened. The two women stayed respectfully by the far wall, and peter stood up without knowing why, except that it was his host who was entering. "Wave been at it for the better part of an hour and still no solution."

"We've been at it for the better part of an hour and still no solution." This was a man toward the end of middle age; although he held his shoulders stiffly back, they looked as if they would sag without a constant effort. His face was lined and tired, and his mouth, like his shoulders, appeared to be falling downward into resignation. He was dressed, as the women were, in a long green robe tied at the waist, and he, too, was barefoot. As he stood in the doorway, with the darkness of the hall behind him, his white head shone softly and his eyes, bright and curious, regarded peter for a long minute before they turned, as the older woman had done, to the crude measuring system on the upper wall. "We are honoured to have you here," he said at last to peter; his voice was resonant, like the sound of the wind in the trees. Without speaking again, he took his seat at the head of the stone table and gestured to peter to take the place on his right. came away from her post by the door and slipped into the place across from peter, and Aunt sima served them all from the iron pot before taking her own place at the foot of the table. peter stared down at the plate before him, and the rich smell of the garlic and meat met him, so that he closed his eyes again for a minute before starting to eat. When he lifted his head he could see, overhead, the dark window; the trees pressed so close against it that their branches were bent against the glass, a tangled crowd of leaves and branches looking in. "What will we call you?" the old man asked peter at last. "I'm peter," peter said, looking only at his plate or up at the window. "And have you come far?" the old man said. "Very far." peter smiled. "I suppose it seems farther than it really is," he explained. peter gathered himself together with an effort. Ever since entering this strange house he had been bewildered, as though drunk from the endless trees he had come through, and uneasy at coming from darkness and the watching forest into a house where he sat down without introductions at his host's table. Swallowing, peter turned to look at gagan, and said, "It's very kind of you to take me in. If you hadn't, I guess I'd have been wandering around in the woods all night." Gagan bowed his head slightly at peter. "I guess I was a little frightened," peter said with a small embarrassed laugh. "All those trees." "Indeed yes," gagan said placidly. "All those trees." peter wondered if he had shown his gratitude adequately. He wanted very much to say something further, something that might lead to an explicit definition of his privileges: whether he was to stay the night, for instance, or whether he must go out again into the woods in the darkness; whether, if he did stay the night, he might have in the morning another such meal as this dinner. When Aunt sima filled his plate a second time, peter smiled up at her. "This is certainly wonderful," he said to her. "I don't know when I've had a meal I enjoyed this much." Aunt sima bowed her head to him as gagan had before. "The food comes from the woods, of course," gagan said. "sima gathers her garlic down by the river, but naturally none of that need concern you." "I suppose not," peter said, feeling that he was not to stay the night. "Tomorrow will be soon enough for you to see the house," gagan added. "I suppose so," peter said, realizing that he was indeed to stay the night. "Tonight," gagan said, his voice deliberately light. "Tonight, I should like to hear about you, and what things you have seen on your journey, and what takes place in the world you have left." peter smiled; knowing that he could stay the night, and could not in charity be dismissed before the morning, he felt relaxed. Aunt sima good dinner had pleased him, and he was ready enough to talk with his host. "I don't really know quite how I got here," he said. "I just took the road into the woods." "You would have to go through the woods to get here," his host agreed soberly. "Before that," peter went on, "I passed a lot of farmhouses and a little town—do you know the name of it? I asked a woman there for a meal and she turned me away." He laughed now, at the memory, with Aunt sima good dinner finished. "And before that," he said, "I was studying." "You are a scholar," the old man said. "Naturally." "I don't know why." peter turned at last to gagan and spoke frankly. "I don't know why," he repeated. "One day I was there, in college, like everyone else, and then the next day I just left, without any reason except that I did." He glanced from gagan to sima; they were all looking at him with blank expectation. He stopped, and said mile, "And I guess that's all that happened before I came here." "He brought a cat with him," sima said softly, her eyes down. "A cat?" gagan looked politely around the kitchen, saw peter cat curled up under the stove, and nodded. "One brought a dog," he said to Aunt sima. "Do you remember the dog?" Aunt sima nodded, her face unchanging. There was a sound at the door, and said without moving, "That is coming for his supper." Aunt sima rose and went over to the outer door and opened it. A cat, tiger-striped where peter cat was black, but about the same size, trotted casually into the kitchen, without a glance for Aunt sima, went directly for the stove, then saw peters cat. "I think they're going to fight," peter said nervously, half rising from his seat. "Perhaps I'd better—" Gagan sighed. "What is your cat's name?" he inquired. "I'm terribly sorry," peter said, with a fleeting fear that the irrational cat might have deprived them both of a bed. "Shall I go and find Gagan laughed. "He was fairly beaten," he said, "and has no right to come back." Now we have a name, Grim, and no cat, so we can give the name to your cat." peter slept that night in a stone room at the top of the house; a room reached by the dark staircase leading from the hall. gagan carried a candle to the room for him, and peters cat, now named Grim, left the warm stove to follow peter. The room was small and neat, and the bed was a stone bench, which peter, investigating after his host had gone, discovered to his amazement was mattresses with leaves, and had for blankets heavy furs that looked like bearskins. "This is quite a forest," peter said to the cat, rubbing a corner of the bearskin between his hands. "And quite a family." Against the window, as against all the windows in the house, was the wall of trees, crushing themselves hard against the glass. "I wonder if that's why they made this house out of stone?" peter asked the cat. "So, the trees wouldn't push it down? All night long the sound and the feeling of the trees crowding against the house came into peters dreams, and he turned gratefully in his sleep to the cat purring beside him in the great fur coverings. In the morning, peter came down into the kitchen, where Aunt sima, in their green robes, were moving about the stove. His cat, who had followed him all the way down the stairs, moved immediately ahead of him in the kitchen to sit under the stove and watch Aunt sima expectantly. When he came, he nodded to peter and they sat, as before, Aunt sima serving them all. did not speak this morning, and when the meal was over, he rose, gesturing to peter to follow him. They went out into the hall, with its silent closed doors, and gagan paused. "You have seen only part of the house, of course," he said. "Our handmaidens keep to the kitchen unless called to this hall." "Where do they sleep?" peter asked. "In the kitchen?" He was immediately embarrassed by his own question, and smiled awkwardly at gagan to say that he did not deserve an answer, but gagan shook his head in amusement and put his hand on peters shoulder. "On the kitchen floor," he said. And then he turned his head away, but peter could see that he was laughing. "Very old," gagan said, as though surprised by the question. "A house was found to be vital, of course." "Of course," peter said, agreeably. "I know I am supposed to be giving you some kind of moral guidance but I just can't get over how weird an ear looks up close. "I know I'm supposed to be giving you some kind of moral guidance, but I just can't get over how weird an ear looks up close." "In here," gagan said, opening one of the two great doors on either side of the entrance. "In here are the records kept." peter followed him in, and gagan went to a candle that stood in its own wax on a stone table and lit it with the flint that lay beside it. He then raised the candle high, and peter saw that the walls were covered with stones, piled up to make loose, irregular shelves. On some of the shelves great, leather-covered books stood, and on other shelves lay stone tablets, and rolls of parchment. "They are of great value," gagan said sadly. "I have never known how to use them, of course." He walked slowly over and touched one huge volume, and then turned to show peter his fingers covered with dust. "It is my sorrow," he said, "that I cannot use these things of great value." peter, frightened by the books, drew back into the doorway. "At one time," gagan said, shaking his head, "there were many more. Many, many more. I have heard that at one time this room was made large enough to hold the records. I have never known how they came to be destroyed." Still carrying the candle, he led peter out of the room and shut the big door behind them. Across the hall another door faced them. As gagan led the way in with the candle, peter saw that it was another bedroom, larger than the one in which he had slept, but with the trees pressing as close against it. He held the candle high again and peter saw a stone bench like his own, with heavy furs lying on it, and above the bed a long and glittering knife resting upon two pegs driven between the stones of the wall. "The keeper of the records," gagan said, and sighed briefly before he smiled at peter in the candlelight. "We are like two friends," he added. "One showing the other his house." Christopher followed him helplessly back into the hall, where gagan blew out the candle and left it on a shelf by the door, and then out the front door to the tiny cleared patch before the house which was surrounded by the stone wall that ran to the road. Although for a small distance before them the world was clear of trees, it was not very much lighter or more pleasant, with the forest only barely held back by the stone wall, edging as close to it as possible, pushing, as peter had felt since the day before, crowding up and embracing the little stone house in horrid possession. He leaned affectionately over the roses, which grew gloriously against the stone of the house, on a vine that rose triumphantly almost to the height of the door. Over him, over the roses, over the house, the trees leaned eagerly. "They need to be tied up against stakes every spring," gagan said. He stepped back a pace and measured with his hand above his head. "A stake—a small tree stripped of its branches will do, and sima will get it and sharpen it—and the rose vine tied to it as it leans against the house." peter nodded. "Someday the roses will cover the house, I imagine," he said. "Do you think so?" gagan turned eagerly to him. "My roses?" "It looks like it," peter said awkwardly, his fingers touching the first stake, bright against the stones of the house. Gagan shook his head, smiling. "Remember who planted them," he said.

They went inside again and through the hall into the kitchen, where Aunt sima stood against the wall as they entered. Again, they sat at the stone table and Aunt sima served them, and again gagan said nothing while they ate and Aunt sima looked down at their plates as always. After the meal was over, gagan bowed to peter before leaving the room, and while Aunt sima cleared the table of plates and cloth peter sat on the bench with his cat on his knee. The women seemed to be unusually occupied. Aunt sima, at the stove, set down iron pots enough for a dozen meals, sent to fetch a special utensil from an alcove in the corner of the kitchen, came back to report that it had been mislaid "since the last time" and could not be found, so that Aunt sima had to put down her cooking spoon and go herself to search. set a great pastry shell on the stone table, and she and Aunt sima filled it slowly and lovingly with spoonsful from one or another pot on the stove, stopping to taste and estimate, questioning each other with their eyes. "What are you making?" peter asked finally. A feast,", glancing at him quickly and then away. Peters cat watched, purring, until Aunt sima disappeared into the kitchen alcove again and came back carrying the trussed carcass of what seemed to peter to be a wild pig. She set this on the spit before the great fireplace, sat beside it to turn the spit. Then peters cat leaped down and ran over to the fireplace to sit beside and taste the drops of fat that fell on the great hearth as the spit was turned. Who is coming to your feast?" peter asked, amused. looked around at him, and Aunt sima half turned from the stove. There was a silence in the kitchen, a silence of no movement and almost no breath, and then, before anyone could speak, the door opened and gagan came in. He was carrying the knife from his bedroom, and he held it out for peter to see with a shrug of resignation. When gagan had seated himself at the table Aunt sima disappeared again into the alcove and brought back a grindstone, which she set before gagan. Deliberately, with the slow caution of a pleasant action lovingly done, gagan set about sharpening the knife. He held the bright blade against the moving stone, turning the edge little by little with infinite delicacy. "You say you've come far?" he said over the sound of the knife, and for a minute his eyes left the grindstone to rest on peter. "Quite a way," peter said, watching the grindstone. "I don't know how far, exactly." "And you were a scholar?" "Yes," peter said. "A student." Gagan looked up from the knife again, to the estimate marked on the wall. When the knife was razor sharp, he held it up to the light from the fire, studying the blade. Then he looked at peter and shook his head humorously. "As sharp as any weapon can be," he said. Aunt sima spoke, unsolicited, for the first time. "Sun's down," she said. Gagan nodded. He looked at for a minute, and then at Aunt sima. Then, with his sharpened knife in his hand, he walked over and put his free arm around for a minute she leaned her back against it, watching peter, and then, standing away from it, she opened it again. peter, staring, walked slowly over to the open door, as Aunt sima seemed to expect he would, and heard behind voice from the hearth. "He'll be down by the river," she said softly. "Go far around and come up behind him." The door shut solidly behind peter and he leaned against it, looking with frightened eyes at the trees that reached for him on either side. Then, as he pressed his back in terror against the door, he heard the voice calling from the direction of the river, so clear and ringing through the trees that he hardly knew it as gagan: "Who is he dares enter these my woods?"

The slumber of woods

One day in deep dark woods a deer was born. His name was limo. His mother washed him all over with her tongue. "limo," she said. "My little limo." The young limo was curious about everything. He learned he was a deer, and so was his mother. He learned there are other deer in the forest, and someday he would meet them. He learned the trails his mother followed were made by the deer. Bugs and critters, sounds and smells. So many wonders to explore! limo A Life in the Woods. Sometimes on a trail, suddenly his mother would stop still. She would open her ears wide and listen from all directions. First- over there! Then- here! Limo would wait. At last, when she said, "It's all right. There's no danger. We can go," then the two of them would start on the trail again. But he did not know why they had to do this. One day, his mother took him to the meadow for the first time. He started to run out to the open clearing but she jumped right in front of him. "Stop!" said she. "Stay here. I must go out first. Wait till I call for you. But if I start to run, you must turn around and run back into the woods very fast. Do not stop. Do you understand me?"

Limos mother, slowly stepped out into the open meadow. She sniffed all around. She looked this way and that, alert and carefully. After a while she said, "It's fine, limo. Nothing to worry about. Come on!" He bounded out to meet her. Oh, what a bright sun! Back in the woods, limo had seen a stray sunbeam every now and then, but here the hot bright sun warmed him all over. He felt marvellous and jumped high into the air. Each time he landed on grass softer than any grass he had ever felt. Then he leaped back up again, over and over. In some places the flowers were so thick, they made a sweet carpet. But what was that tiny thing dancing in the air? "Look, Mother!" said limo. "The flower is flying." Why, that flower must have needed to dance so much, limo thought, that it broke right off its stem to rise up and dance in the air. "That's not a flower, limo," said the mother, "it's a butterfly." Then — Thump, thump, thump! On a rock was a young hare, a rabbit, thumping its foot. "Hello, there!" smiled Hare, raising one tall ear. "Want to play?" "Sure!" said limo "Catch me!" Hare hopped off the rock into the grass, hop-hopping away. Limo was a bit faster at running and jumping, but Hare was better at hiding, so the two of them had a fine time. On top of the flowers, a tall, fluffy black and white tail was sliding over to them. "Why, I'd know that tail anywhere!" said Hare. "It's my friend Skunk. He's under the flowers. Skunk?" And sure enough, a black and white head popped up. "This is limo," said Hare. Soon the three of them were exploring the meadow, sniffing its rich deep smells. After a while, Hare and Skunk had to go home. Limo looked around. "Mother! Where are you?" At the far side of the meadow he saw her, with a creature that looked just like her. "limo, come meet my sister Ena," called Bambi's mother. "And her two little ones. limo hopped over. Two fawns, little Feline and her brother Leo, were running in and out of their mother's legs. Feline gave a leap and landed right in front of limo, then jumped back to Leo. With care, limo stepped up to her. Feline hopped off to one side and Leo followed. Soon the three of them were chasing each other up and down the grass.

"Now run off and play, all of you," said limos, mother. Every day after that, the three young deer played and chattered. They raced and chased, they nibbled many strawberries and blueberries on the bushes, and sometimes they just talked. One day, limo said, "Do you know what danger means?" Something very bad," whispered Leo. But what is it?" said limo. I know what danger is," said Feline. It's what you run away from." But soon they were chasing and playing again. Limo mother and Ena came up. "Come on now," they said. "It's time to go home." Far off at the top of a hill two large proud deer came into view, with enormous heads of antlers. Turning to them, Feline said, "Who are they? Those are your fathers," said Ena. "If you are smart and don't run into danger," said limos mother to her son, "someday you will grow up as big and handsome as your father. And you will have antlers, too." Limos heart swelled with pride. As limo grew, he learned how to sniff the air. He could tell if his friend Hare was coming, or if a fox had just trotted by. He could tell if it would rain soon. One afternoon came a raging storm. Lightning flashed and thunder crashed. Limo thought the end of the world had come. But when he lay by his mother's side, he felt safe. One day when limo wandered about in the woods, he came upon a sharp, unpleasant smell. Curious, he followed it. It led to a clearing, where stood a strange creature. He had never seen such a creature. It stood up on its rear legs, and in its two arms it held something long and black — could it be a third leg? The smell of the creature somehow filled him with terror. The creature raised its long black arm. In a flash, limos mother rushed up to him. "Run, limo, run! As fast as you can!" Limos mother bounded over shrubs and bushes. He kept pace beside her till they were back at their leafy home. Later, limos mother said, "Did you see the Human?" limo nodded yes. That's the one who brings danger," she said. And both of them shuddered. Limo was still growing. The first time he woke to find his mother gone from his side, he was scared. It was early morning and still dark. "Mother! Mother!" he called out. A large shadow approached, bigger than his mother's. Standing before a pool of moonlight, a Great Old Buck looked proud and stern. "Who are you calling?" said the Buck with a frown. "Can't you take care of yourself?" limo did not dare answer. He lowered his head in shame. "Look up," said the Old Buck, "Listen to me. Watch. Smell. Find out for yourself. You will be fine on your own." The leaves fell and limo grew even taller. His mother started leaving him alone more and more, letting him meet other deer and creatures of the forest. Feline, Leo, Hare and Skunk were still limo best friends, but he also found other creatures fascinating to watch and sometimes fun to play with. One wet winter day, the terrible smell of Humans swept across the forest. The scent was so strong that there had to be many Humans in a group! Most animals quickly fled out of danger. But some were not as lucky. With the hunter's loud noise and great power, many animals were killed and one of them was limos mother. After that terrible day, limo felt lost. He wandered about. How could this awful thing have happened? Suddenly, the Great Old Buck stepped out in front of him. "Were you out in the meadow when it happened?" the Old Buck said. And you're not calling for your mother?" said the Buck. Suddenly limo felt full of courage. "I can take care of myself!" he said, looking up. The Great Old Buck smiled. "Listen to me," he said. "Smell. Watch. Learn to live and be careful. Find out for yourself. Now farewell." And he vanished into the deep forest. Winter came. Strong and bitter cold winds swept through the woods. Deep snow covered the forest floor. There was little food to eat. limo felt hungry and cold all the time. Nearly all the bark on the trees had been peeled away by hungry deer. Still, the cold wind blistered on, day after day. Leo had always been smaller than limo and Feline. He shivered all the time. He could hardly stand up anymore. One day a flock of crows flew overhead, yelling loudly. "Caw! Caw!" The geese also screamed in the sky, "Gawk! Gawk!" They warned of the Humans coming - again! Hare hopped up and down in alarm. "We're surrounded! They are everywhere!" A single boom crashed like thunder, and one goose fell from the sky. All the animals ran like mad, even the tiny tit mouse. Another short crash like thunder, and a fox fell down on the forest floor. Bang! Bang! Hare called out to limo, "We have to get out of here!" limo and Hare started to bound away. But was that Leo, lying in the snow? Another young deer bounded by. "limo, run! Don't just stand there if you can run!" He took off like the wind, and as limo ran along, he called behind him, "I will come back for you, Leo!" limo ran and ran. Soon the sound that boomed as loud as thunder grew more and more distant. When limo returned to where Leo had been, there was no trace of him, not even his tracks. Just big tracks. Feline and her mother were pacing around the spot. "What has become of him?" wailed Ena. But they all knew. They could smell it. A Human had come and had taken Leo away. Weeks passed. At last, little sprigs of fresh green grass popped up through the snow. Then more and more tufts of green. What was left of the snow melted away. As the trees and bushes turned green and the weather warmed, all the animals started to act so oddly. Birds flitted about two by two. So many creatures large and small were in pairs. His friend Skunk spent all his time was with a girl skunk and hardly noticed limo. Even his friend Hare seemed in a daze, forever staring at a girl hare and thumping his foot.

"What's happened to my friends?" said limo. I am alone." There was a rustling in the leaves behind him. There stood Feline, but she was grown up now, like he was. Each of them was thinking, "How different you look!" They gazed at each other and smiled. "It has been a long time since we saw each other," said Feline. "Do you remember all the berries on the bushes we ate?" said the other. The two seemed to understand each other perfectly. A fat deer came up to them, sniffing the air. "Sister, don't you know me?" Feline and limo turned in amazement. "Leo!" They rushed up to him in joy. Leo told his story. "I was with a Human. I have seen a lot more than the rest of you, all together." Dogs had found him when he lay in the snow, and they barked. The Human came and carried Leo to the place where he lived. "It was as warm as summer inside," said Leo. "Rain may pour outside, but not inside where Humans live. It is always dry and warm! And there is always something to eat, too - turnips, hay, potatoes, carrots - yum!" No, the Human wouldn't hurt me. If he loves you, or if you serve him, he's good to you,". "They all loved me there. The children petted me." The Great Old Buck strode out from the bushes. "What kind of band is that you have on your neck?" It's a halter I wear," "It's a great honour to wear the Human's halter." Be silent!" said the Great Old Buck. "You poor thing." He turned and was gone. One day when Leo and limo were together, they smelled the scent of a Human. "We must hide, at once!" No need for that," "The Humans know me." Then all at once a sharp bang! And Leo fell down. Fortunately, the Human never came after Leo. Instead, when the scent of the Human went away, limo pulled his friend to a leafy place where he could rest and be out of danger. Limo knew what weeds his mother used to eat to heal a wound faster. As he brought the weeds to Leo. he wondered, "Why must this always happen to us?" limo thought of the Great Old Buck who had said, "Find out for yourself." Find out what? Feline and Ena brought Leo food and visited with him for hours. Limo often came by, too, until Leo was healed. The words from the Great Old Buck still fresh in his head — "Learn to live and be careful." Limo was starting to understand. Seasons came and went. Limo grew still taller. His antlers were nearly full grown now. One day, limo caught a new warning smell in the air. It was a hot and smoky smell. A flock of crows rushed overhead, cawing loudly. Fire! At once, the animals were running, running, as fast as they could. It wasn't easy to run away from fire. Sometimes it seemed to rush in from different directions. After hours went by of flames and smoke, the fire started to wind down at last. The smell of fire was fading, too. "Do not be frightened," said the Old Buck. Closer and closer they went to the village. "Look, limo," he said. There in front of them were dozens of huts. Each one was burned, some almost to the ground, others burned mostly on the roof. The village was empty. "You see, limo," said the Old Buck. "The houses of the Humans get burned by fire just like the places where we stay in the woods. The Human isn't above us. We are just the same. Do you understand me, limo?"

"Fire burns the woods where we live, and it burns the villages of Humans, too," said limo. "We are not so different from Humans." We both live under the same great powers in this world," said the Great Old Buck. "Now I can go," said the Great Old Buck. "Don't follow me. My time is up. Goodbye my son, I loved you so."

Now limo had become a full Buck himself. His antlers spiked and gleamed in the sun. Sometimes he would visit the corner of the woods where he had spent his childhood. Some of the trails were still there. Once while wandering there he saw Leo and his sister, Feline. When he saw Feline, his heart beat faster. He wanted to rush to her. He gazed after her. Finally, she was gone. Then he heard the call of two little fawns.

"Can't you stay by yourselves?" said limo. The little brother and sister were too much in awe of the great Buck to answer. Limo thought, this little fellow pleases me. He reminds me of the deer face I used to see when I looked in the brook years ago. Perhaps I'll meet him again. The little girl is nice, too. Feline looked like that once. Listen to me," said limo to the two fawns. "You must watch and listen. Find out for yourself. You will be fine on your own." This leads her to become suspicious and she tries to talk to Marcy about it. But Marcy acts strangely, and is shadowed by one of the teachers. Soon after, Heather finds Marcy's bed empty and covered in leaves. Later, she is confronted in the woods by Samantha, who reveals that she has actually been trying to protect Heather with her antics. She tells Heather that the school is led by a coven of witches who want to take all of the girls away. Samantha explains that she has called Heather's father to help her escape and that the milk is poisoned. The girls are both caught by a school mistress, who promptly takes Samantha away. Samantha is later found hanging from a bedsheet in the cafeteria. When a police officer comes to investigate, Heather tells him of the missing students. The officer confronts the headmistress, but she claims that the girls ran away. Another mistress "leads" the officer into the woods to find the girls, where he is killed by the living vines of a tree. Heather's parents show up to take her home, though the headmistress tries to persuade them otherwise. On the way home, their car is mysteriously flipped and Heather is knocked unconscious. Alice is dragged out of the car by a living vine and kicks Joe in the head, knocking him out. Heather and Joe wake up in a nearby hospital. Before they can reach each other, Ms. Traverse has Heather dragged away, then slits her own hand and forces her black blood down Joe's throat, which puts him into a catatonic state. Heather returns to the school in despair. She drinks the milk that evening, but later vomits it back up, finding tree bark in it. Back at the hospital, Joe wakes up and vomits up Ms. Traverse's black blood, which also has tree bark in it. He quickly escapes and goes to find Heather. That night, Heather begins to hear voices again, and when she attempts to leave, a living vine captures her. When she awakens, she is wrapped in vines in a large foggy room, next to Ann and Marcy, who are also held captive. All of the teachers appear and reveal themselves to be witches. Ms. Traverse is their leader, and she explains that their spirits have been trapped in the woods all these years, and they need to inhabit the bodies of young women to escape their imprisonment. Heather appears to be the centrepiece of her plan because she has the strongest powers among the gifted students. Heather is coerced into completing the ritual, and the vines begin to mummify all of the girls in the school. Before it can complete itself, Joe breaks into the room with an and begins to kill the witches. Heather breaks free from the vines and grabs the, proceeding to chop all of the witches into pieces. Heather and Joe then leave with all of the girls, walking down the road into the daylight as the school burns in the distance behind them. When we rise, every day of our lives. What do we have in our minds? What makes us rise and get up with abundant, less or no enthusiasm. With whatever thought we rise or whatever sort of behaviour we have, we rise but why do we? An urge to enhance and mount up and see what a new day of life can be, makes me open my eyes and look at the sun shining through my window shouting-

"I'm shining a bit more today; you want to see me in my new style" Yup, you are wondering right the sun doesn't talk to me nor will I like to but when I say this to myself that I need to get up and see this day, I have to. And one day just like this I got up. With no plans as to how I need to spend this day. First thing I rang up my friends- "Dude this is insane, I feel energetic. Want to go for a trek up the hill with Sam?" Cool, good idea, the sun isn't that hard today feels cool, lets, do it at eleven in the morning?" Eleven in the morning? Have you gone nuts? Of course, in the night, it scary and much better, isn't it? Got it? "You will call up Sam?" I asked excitedly I spend the next two hours surfing through the internet for the required items and then marched down the street to pick up the necessities there. It was ten o'clock in the night and I was ready with all the requirements in our bag pack for the day. I then trooped alone into the streets of Claret; it was the street on which the hill was located. It stood up: tall and giant like a monster in night. I crawled my way into the sealed thoroughfare and saw Sam waiting for m "Hey!" She yelled from the distant Quiet, no one has to know that we are here" I said reaching nearer to her We heard footsteps and saw Clara waiting for us at the sealed thoroughfare she had bought Cynthia, an Australian girl whose parents were world travellers and bloggers, she lived with her aunt and had exceptional knowledge about everything. Everything we didn't know about. She came and we greeted her with warmness and started our journey deep into the darkness. Soon we reached a spot on the hill which had three ways going: north, west and south. We choose north and went ahead. It was three in the night when we enlightened the fire and camped around it. Cynthia was very helpful. She was a sweet and a kind girl, helping each step in the trek till the end. We sat around the fire and tried to keep the flames as low and invisible as possible, if anyone found out that we here, in the woods it was impossible if we were kept alive. I still wondered if I could know the mystery behind the woods, why were these sealed. And suddenly it struck- "Cynthia, you shall know a lot about these woods tell us why were these sealed" It's a long story Kiara" she addressed me "I don't know about it much but will tell you all sheer knowledge I have." She spoke. I finished and her jaw dropped, she was astounded "I feel this is unbelievable, I have no idea about it, you know knowing things without my parents around is tough, by the way let's go to sleep now" We entered our tents, two had been set up, in the first one: Cynthia and I were sleeping while in the other were Sam and Clara. We talked a bit more and slept, the minute she put down her head onto the ground she spiked up with pain, shouting. Cynthia since that night had wrapped herself with silence, we don't know what she thought, what pieces of knowledge she connected in her mind and cried. All things aside, days passed quickly and the security near the hill intensified. But the truth was still unanswered- What had happened in the mystery wood? Chilled Autumn air settled over me, the dryness of it tickling my lungs. I walked down the dirt path, overtaken by tree roots and layered with crisp, fallen foliage. I kept my head down and shoulders hunched for most of the walk, searching for the leaves that would make the most satisfying crunch when I stepped on them. When I removed my hands from my coat pockets the harshness of the air prickled my fingers. I finally brought my head up and evened out my posture. The cemetery gate was slightly askew, silently enticing me to enter. The people buried here didn't have many visitors anymore, the most recent year on any gravestone was 1850. Nature had reclaimed the forlorn cemetery as her own—some headstones had toppled over, and most had become overgrown and faded. On one evening visit with my sister Louise, we saw forget-me-nots placed over one of the graves. I searched for clues of their origin, but the inscription on the headstone did nothing but further my curiosity. Like most, it was almost completely deteriorated, only visible to those who looked.

No last name. Nothing about her family, the life she lived, or who she was. Years have passed since I saw the forget-me-nots on Abigail's grave, and I still wonder if or when the flowers will appear again. I walked about the cemetery, collecting the brightest botanicals I could find. I recalled their scientific names from a grade school expedition: acer rubrum, monarda didymo, lobelia cardinalis. I used a long piece of switchgrass to tie my makeshift bouquet together, and held it up to the sun, admiring how the crimson edges burned in the light—before placing it over Abigail's grave. Autumn whipped up another bluster of brisk air, and I turned and exited the cemetery as the wind echoed at my back. On my way home, I was joined by Prince, the shaggy black Maine Coon that occasionally accompanied me on my walks. His coat was dusty. Leaves clung to his belly, and tufts of fur stuck out from under his ears, but he walked with reality. And why should he not? It was his kingdom, and I was merely an inhabitant.

"Hello, your highness. How are you today?" I asked him, with the air of respect one of royal lineage deserved. I often kept treats in my coat pocket as tribute to his rule. Prince stopped walking, looked up at me, slowly blinked, then continued on. It was his usual response, but it still warmed my heart each time he did it.

When I got home, Louise was sitting in her usual spot by the window. Her shoulders were slouched forward and she held her volume of Edgar Allan Poe short stories too close to her face. We turned the street corner and the house came into view. It looked less like a castle than I remembered, but seeing it again gave me chills. The chipping paint I remembered was stripped away, the result of recent preservation work. The windows, however, were the same— they still evoked the intrigue I had felt since childhood. Louise gently tugged my arm. "This is it," she said, and I sensed a hint of wonder in her eyes. I walked down the hallway until I came across the open basement door. The basement was well lit with a harsh LED glow, and there were a few worn chairs arranged around an obtrusive metal desk. On the desk was a haphazard pile of papers, files, and manilla envelopes. "There's a bunch of information about the house in here," Louise said while squinting at the binder. We skimmed through the weighty binder, flipping through pictures and descriptions of the house's collections: dining room chairs, the grandfather clock in the parlour, a taxidermized owl—a black and white photograph caught my attention. I flipped back to the page. It was the painting I saw upstairs. Underneath, a small the next day, Louise and I walked along the familiar path overtaken with roots and leaves. Prince greeted us at the cemetery gate, stretching out his front paws towards us, as though bowing. I placed the forget-me-nots over Abigail's grave and rested my hand lightly over the top, closing my eyes and breathing in the freedom of the forest. We sat in the grass, wanting to be with her, with Abigail. The wind picked up, cold air rushing past us, and we walked home. She came to stay in this sweet little guest house at the edge of the woods. There were mountains all around and the air was wonderfully crisp and fresh. She had come here solely for her convalescing aunt who needed some good change. It was a tiny little hamlet with cottages scattered about. She made her aunt comfortable and went to look for the caretaker. "Could we have some tea, please?" Yes, I was just about to bring it for you along with some snacks. You must be hungry after the journey. Just give me a second." She went to the window to see the countryside. It looked so beautiful. A carpet of grass with floral designs! She had never seen so many tiny red, violet and yellow flowers. She smiled. The caretaker entered with the tray. The aroma of hot samosas and sandwiches stirred a rumbling in her stomach and her mouth began to water instantly.

"You can see we are a small community here and if you get lost, it would be difficult to search you out." Seema, please don't do anything foolish and return while it's bright." She took her little dog, Pinto with her. He merrily ran ahead and barked at some small mole or badger hiding behind the bush. She was in a trance looking at so many flowers. The sun was still up and the rays pushed their way through the thick foliage. "Pinto......come here," she whistled. He came scampering on his tiny feet. They walked together and entered the woods. She could hear the flow of water. Was it a spring or a stream? She stepped carefully over the stones to come to the clearing. What a pretty sight! The trees created a canopy beneath which a little river flowed. And then she saw the golden swans. A flock of them white as snow! She stared at them totally fascinated. She moved forward with her hands extended hoping that they would come to her. They flapped their large wings and slowly lifted themselves up. Pinto stood silently watching the scene. He didn't even bark! The swans flew away and with them the sun seemed to fade away.

Seema knew it was time to return but the waft of fragrance stopped her. She saw the shrubs of white lilies growing up the slope. Should she quickly go and pluck a few? She loved lilies. She started forward when she heard Pinto barking at something along But Pinto started moving forward. Before he could go any further, Seema caught up with him and picked him up.

"No, your naughty doggy!" she said. "Come on, let's go home." She started to leave but then again turned and looked at those lilies longingly. Should she try and go to the flowers? They weren't very far away. She took a step forward to go to the shrub when Pinto gave a sudden growl. "What is it?" said Seema. She heard the growl again. She decided to leave the lilies alone for the time being and return to the cottage. Auntie may start worrying. She needed to pluck the flowers urgently. But she knew that it was incorrect to pluck flowers in the night. It disturbed their sleep. She had to do it and she was sure the flowers would forgive her. Tomorrow her father was to come and she wanted to make a garland to welcome him. She hurried out of the gate. In the bright moonlight, she easily made her way to the forest. She knew the way and she half ran half walked to it. It was dark within the forest but it was full of noises. The shooting of an owl was frightening but the song of the nightingale put her at ease. She screwed her eyes to see the path. She came to the little rivulet. The swans were there with their graceful necks tucked in for they were fast asleep. She felt terrible, she didn't want to disturb anyone. She picked up her skirts and started her climb. The fragrance told her where the lilies were exactly. She quickly reached up and started plucking the flowers. She tucked them in her stole and some she carried in her hand. Something cold touched her elbow and she jumped out of her skin. It was a little deer.... a fawn. It was a baby. Dear God! Had it lost its mother? The eyes were looking so large and innocent. Her heart melted. The skin was light beige and the spots shone like go There was a rustle of leaves. Leaves that were being tread upon as someone walked. Who could be here? A wolf howled far away in the forest seemed to howl. She swallowed. The tiny fawn turned and began to run. She ran after it. What if it fell and hurt itself? The footsteps could now be heard clearly. Who was following her? As the started to climb up the slope, she had to pick up her long skirt. What was she wearing? A long brown skirt? It was so heavy to handle. She could sense the person behind. She half turned to see the shadow of the man still hidden in the trees. She panted as she quickly climbed up. A rifle shot rent the air and the silence was shattered. The birds cackled, the animals yelled and the little fawn shivered beside her. She stood in her place. Her long skirt hid the timid animal "Heel," said the man. The dogs obeyed, sheathing their ugly teeth. They wagged their tail. "I have to take care of this unnecessary interruption." He started to take steps towards her. "Stop," she said, "stay where you are." He man stopped and raised his eyebrows. "Are you ordering me? Me?" He shrugged and continued his walk. She picked up the fawn and began to run. He caught her and turned her around. He took the fawn out of her clutching hands and dropped it to the ground

"Just gathering food for me and my friends here. They can have you while I can make a good dinner of him." He looked down at the fawn who was huddled next to her. The wicked smile, the cruel words showed the man was indeed the devil. She gasped as if she was being choked. She was fighting for her breath, her lashes dropped but her hands remained tightly closed.

Seema woke up with a start. Her forehead was wet with sweat and her breathing was ragged. Her heart was thudding and she was shivering out of dread. But...but.... where was she? She was safe in her bed. Oh God! It had been a scary dream. She sighed with relief. She took a towel and wiped her face. She lay back. She turned on her side, and put her hands under her head. As she sleepily thought about what had happened, she got the mild whiff of lilies. Where were the lilies? She frowned. She opened her palms and slowly smelled them. The fragrance of the lilies was coming from her palms. She gasped in shock! How could this be? She hadn't even touched the lilies.........eve given up so much outdoor recreation this year. Not that we're mad about it. Saving lives matters more than backpacking trips and summer marathons. But as the days get warmer, I feel myself craving the smoke-in-my hair smell from a campfire. I miss the sound of owls, the dwindling supply of beer in the cooler, and the way time suspends as you wait for the flames to die.

Mostly, though, I miss the stories. There's something about the light of the fire in the backcountry darkness that makes you lean in and listen a little closer. And, of course, a few sips of whiskey never hurt a good tall tale.

We can't bring back your spring campfires with friends. We can, however, bring our favourite campfire stories to you. Save these three for retelling when things return to normal—or tell them now over a Zoom call with your friends. The Ghost of Oxford Milford Road He killed the engine and flashed his lights three times. "No joke, there was a single headlight that appeared three-quarters of a mile down the road," Culp says. "You saw it start to come, going pretty slow. It kept coming and coming. My wife was freaking out. It was coming closer and closer." As a collision seemed imminent, Culp turned on his car's lights. He expected to see a kid on a bike, bailing out from his prank now that he'd been caught. "But there's nothing there. The light is just gone," he says. They got out of the car. They walked around, trying to figure out what it was they could have seen. "To this day, we still talk about it. I saw something I cannot explain," he says. If you get him and his wife around a campfire, they'll swear up and down that the story is true. And if you're ever in Oxford, Ohio, consider parking for just a few minutes on Oxford Milford Road at night to test your own nerve. Doug Averill grew up as one of eight boys on his parents' sprawling dude ranch, the Flathead Lake Lodge, in rural Montana. As a teen, the Averill boys ran wild. "We rode around as a little gang of cowboys," he remembers. They'd saddle up and head off to check cattle on the three giant tracts of land the family managed, which formed a triangle around some of the state's most remote rangelands. There, on the ground, were three dead cows neatly arranged in a circle. No obvious wounds were visible, but their reproductive organs had been removed. "But there was never any blood. It was almost surgical removal," Averill remembers. During this decade, America was obsessed with aliens, and write-ups in the local newspapers posited that perhaps this was the work of extra-terrestrials. People mused that aliens had taken the reproductive organs for testing. But one day, Averill and his friends came across a lance in their path. Attached to it was a cryptic note with a threatening message. "That's when we thought, it's got to be people doing this," he says. Then things got really strange. Over the next few days, a series of odd events unfolded. First, the brothers stopped in at a local bar to grab a hamburger, leaving their horses in the back of a stock truck. The horses were packed in tightly, and the Averill's were only gone for a few minutes. When they came back, the horse packed into the middle of the truck was mysteriously out—with no signs of a struggle. "We had no idea how they possibly could have gotten that horse unloaded without unloading all the others," he says.

The next day, a new wrangler on the ranch fell off his horse and was badly injured. They'd all been riding together, but not a single other member of the crew saw the accident. "It was the weirdest thing," Averill says. The man's injuries were so severe that he was left permanently disabled.

Finally, the last terrible thing happened. An old camp cook drove out to meet the brothers and ride for a day. But when he arrived, the tailgate on his stock truck had somehow gone missing, even though it had been there when he'd loaded up. His horse, Betsy, had fallen out of the truck and been dragged behind the vehicle for who knows how long. They had to put her down on the spot. "To be honest, it just killed him to see what had happened to Betsy. We probably should have put him down, too," remembers Averill. "Those three events were just boom, boom, boom—three things in a row that were so weird all tied together, because they were right after we saw that spear," he remembers. Three things: like the three dead cows left in a circle. Averill used to tell the stories from that summer around the campfire quite a lot. But over the years, he's gotten new stories, and so they've been shifted out of rotation. Besides, they're awfully grim. But he recently got a call about a downed bull, a buffalo. It was out in one of the most remote parts of his ranch. "A neighbour had seen a pack of 16 wolves, and normally, wolves don't bother buffalo, but 16 of them? I thought, Well, maybe." He went to investigate. There, lying in a snow-covered field, was the bull. But there were no bullet holes or teeth marks or gashes on its corpse. Even stranger, scavenging animals and birds hadn't touched it. "Not even the buzzards, which is really unusual," he says. One other thing was amiss: its reproductive organs were gone. Ask Averill whether he thinks he's dealing with aliens or humans, and he'll tell you he's pretty sure it's humans. "But I'd rather it was aliens," he adds. After that summer back in the sixties, seeing what humans were capable of, he'd pick aliens any day. Throughout Latin America, you'll hear variations of the story of La Llorona, or the wailing woman. Sometimes she's lost her husband. Sometimes she's lost her children. Sometimes it's both. But in La Parva, a ski spot in the Chilean Andes, the wailing woman is named Lola, and everyone in the area swears they knew her before she died. "A local restaurant owner said he dated her," pro skier Drew Take says, adding that the ski patroller he heard the story from pointed at the exact hut where this tale takes place.

The story starts on a nice day in peak ski season. Lola and her young son planned to spend the day on the slopes. "As can happen in the Andes, a thick fog rose up from the valley, which often precedes the arrival of a real storm. The clouds enveloped the two as they were making their way down from the top of the mountain, and they lost contact with one another," Take says.

Desperate to find her son, Lola began screaming his name as she ran through the thick fog. Unable to see clearly, though, she stumbled down a steep slope and began sliding toward a rocky couloir.

"By chance, a local lift operator who was returning to his cabin came across her body. He was afraid she was dead, but on closer inspection, he found she was still alive, just barely," Take says. Her body was covered in lacerations from sharp rocks, and the only word she said—in the faintest whisper—was her son's name.

The lift operator worked to carefully pull her body to his cabin, which was just up the hill. He bandaged her cuts as best he could and then ran to fetch the doctor. Together the doctor and lift operator made their way back to his hut, the fog hanging thickly in the air. When they arrived, though, the bed was empty. Just the bloody sheets remained.

"Neither the woman nor her son was ever found," Take says. But locals report hearing her wail for her child whenever they're near that lift operator's cabin.

The end

Contents